Ava Schreiber

Voices

story.one – Life is a story

story.one

1st edition 2023
© Ava Schreiber

Production, design and conception:
story.one publishing - www.story.one
A brand of Storylution GmbH

Font set from Minion Pro, Lato and Merriweather.

© Cover photo: Photo by Robert Tudor on Unsplash

Editor: Corinne Alyssa Klarmann

ISBN: 978-3-7108-4080-7

"Reality doesn't always give us the life that we desire, but we can always find what we desire between the pages of books." —Adelise M. Cullens

For you

CONTENT

To get out of the chaotic real world
And into an even more chaotic one

Chapter 1

The room was flooded with people. They were standing in long lines before the food dispensers, sitting in small groups, talking to each other, playing boardgames and eating lunch. I was sitting at a table near to a big glass wall through which I could see a little, blue river, which ran through the school area, and was surrounded by colourful trees and bushes. I sat in the cafeteria alone, reading a German book called "Weil der Welt alles egal ist", in English it's "Because the world doesn't care". I was completely focused on the words and sunken into the less chaotic world with the real world continuing around me. After a while I glanced up into the sunlight which shined through the class into my face and made the surrounding situation look less chaotic and friendlier. I wasn't good with interaction, especially interaction with people, animals are fine because they just listen even though you don't have anything important to say. "Reindeers are better than people, Sven don't you think that's true?", I hummed while looking around to find what made me look up and get out of the familiar world of books and stories.

Nothing has changed from before, except that there were a couple of new people and new groups formed. The rest was normal, like every day in school after lessons. But still, I had this feeling that it wasn't just the sun putting me back into real life. I heard the buzz of people talking, but something was different. Not normal and just unsettling. I closed my eyes for a short time, to block out my eyesight and to just concentrate on the sounds.

Then I heard something, that made a shiver run down my neck, down my back and made my body hair stand up. My hands hold onto a pencil and spun it around like a drumstick, so that I was kept busy. I was able to smell the pasta with tomato sauce, which the person sitting next to me, ate. I could feel my back getting pressed against my chair, feel a slight breeze when a door at the other end of the room opened.

More voices of students and teachers were raining down on me and I heard each footstep of the boy walking across the big room to a table where his friends waited and waved at him.

But then there was the unsettling feeling again, and I noticed something new, something I had never heard before. Voices which weren't produced in the cafeteria or the room next doors or anywhere else close by.

They sprouted in my head and filled it with a cloud. They weren't clear enough to be understood yet, but clear enough to fill my entire head. It was like a brumming, a humming, a song recorded with a broken microphone.

And then I heard a scream. A scream that made the world around me crumble, me shiver and made the people who heard it, feel the pain that caused it.

Chapter 2

My entire body trembled with pain and I could feel how my hope, my will to live, all of that got less and less. The inside screamed, my outside trembled, and I fell from my chair, hit the ground and almost blacked out. "Hey, hey, are you good?", someone asked, but I couldn't answer. I held onto the table and sat up, still hearing the voices and the horrible scream. It felt like the cold, stone floor crumbled under my body into a white, cloudy darkness.

The boy who asked me earlier, if I was OK, jumped and was with two fast steps, next to me. "OK, it's fine. Come!", he said while taking my hand and pulling me upright. I turned my head and realised, that when I looked at north-west, the cloud in my head got smaller and less filling, the pain got less and the voices got less chaotic and more structured. Students were looking and asking questions. "Are you OK? What happened? Do you need help?", all of that was really nice, and I would have felt good and relieved, but I couldn't with the cloud still stopping most of my thoughts. The Pasta-Boy took my by the arm and supported me. The crowd slitted, so that we could pass through without problems and go out of the cafeteria, which we did. Up the stairs and to the secretariat where they asked me what was going on. On the way there, the voices got clearer and the scream faded away slowly and when we arrived at the door of the office, the scream was gone, I could think easily, and I turned to the Pasta-Guy. "Hey, sorry 'bout that. I don't know what happened. I think I blacked out for a minute. Thank you so much for your help!", I said to him, and he smiled, "What's your name?" "Josh, my name is Josh. How about yours?", Josh asked. "Lara", I answered while looking around. The corridor led to the principal's office at the far end and on the sides, new rooms and corridors parted of and would lead into the bathrooms or the stairways. It smelted fresh, and a light breeze touched my scion softly. "Hey, Josh, I'm fine. I don't need anyone to pick me up. So can we just go and forget what happened?", I asked and looked directly in his eyes, to see his reaction. Normally people who have just met another person would be like: OK and walk off. People are not really kind to others when the other person is new, but I could see that Josh was concerned and didn't want me to just go away. "Please, I'm fine.", I said again and Josh nodded. "OK, but be careful. If anything is wrong, text me. Here's my number!" He wrote his telephone number on a piece of paper and handed it to me. I took it with a smile, turned away and ran down the corridor, through a door on the right side, took the staircase left and ran down to my bike.

The screaming had fully stopped, and the voices were no longer a mix, but clear and one after one. I wasn't able to make out what they said, because my heart pounded hard after the running, but what I could hear, was that there were three voices, they were weak and young, like voices of children in the age of maybe 11 or 13.

I unlocked my bike, hopped on and pedalled fast and with the most of my strength. The trees surrounding the road were flashing flocks of green and the houses standing on the side were dark and cold, like the house in front which I stopped. On an old, wooden sign, painted in red, was written: Orphanage Summer. I had arrived at home!

Chapter 3

The ceiling was a huge painting of the blue, night sky, but after years of children living inside the halls and rooms, the paint had started to peel off. My body lay on the hard mattress like a flower swimming on the surface of a lake. How it must feel to just float, glaring up into the beautiful sky, breathing the fresh air of nature and just being. I had spent two hours listening to the voices in my head, trying to understand what they said, to get a clue if they were real or if I was just hallucinating. „Floating, words, what are you trying to say?!", I mumbled to myself and I could feel how smoke came out of my ears after all the thinking. Thump! My roommates Emma and Isabella stormed through the door, exhausted after a day of school, but laughing. „Hey mate! What're you doing?", Emma asked with a smile on her lips. „Oh, I'm running a marathon, don't you see?", I said with sarcasm and Isabella laughed even more. „OK, OK, we are gonna let you run your marathon. See you later!" and as fast as they came in, they were out again.

But now I was out of the world I was in for thinking and couldn't get back that easily. I sat up with my back to the wall on which the beds stood and looked around. There was a small window with light blue curtains and a round table on which we did our homework. The walls were full of pictures, either drawings other children here drew or pictures we drew or took. It was colourful and always nice to look at. A clock hang over the red door at the north-west side of my room. That's when I decided to stand up and go out because I realised that it was dinner time. I had been lying in bed for two hours, so that it was 6 o'clock in the evening, which meant: Time to eat!

Step after step I made my way through the messy room (because well, three teenage girls lived there), through the coloured door and right when I stepped outside onto the corridor I heard it.

„Where do you think we are?" „I think near Manchester"

A map, starting and ending points, positions, hours of travelling, forms of travelling. A stream of pictures and information formed in my head and somehow the corridor felt like it was getting smaller, and I felt like I was stuck somehow, somewhere, in a form of prison made up by my own mind and body. My feet couldn't hold my weight any more and I broke down. I slid down the brick wall, played with the soft corner of my old t-shirt without realising it and looking into nothingness while trying to figure out the fastest way to get to Manchester. These voices in my head weren't a sign of me being paranoid or crazy, no these voices were voices of real people, and I was able to feel, that something was off and that the keepers of the voices were in danger. So there was only one reasonable thing to do.

„I need to go to Manchester!"

Chapter 4

It was 8 o'clock when dinner was over, and I had arrived back in my room, where Emma and Isabella were sitting in their beds, reading and learning for school. The voices had faded away while dinner, so that I was able to check out a map of the subway here in London, on my phone. With the train and subway and some other vehicles the trip would be about 3 hours long. Because I had been doing different kinds of jobs in the holidays, I had made enough money to buy tickets for bus, train and even be able to sleep in a hotel for maybe a day. And that was my plan, I would skip lessons and just run away because not one would care. The people in school never even noticed me and here in this hole of rubbish, called an orphanage, the only people who might miss me, would be Emma and Isabella. I took my green-brown backpack, which I normally used when I had a sport event, and looked around the room full of stuff. There was old clothing lying around, school books piled up next to the tables and somehow, I didn't know how and didn't want to know, there was a cushion of the sofa from the room next doors. My foot stepped on one of Emma's shoes, my other one on a notebook, but I managed to get to the group closet. In there were the cleaned clothes stacked on top of each other and my hands grabbed clean t-shirts of various colours but mostly camouflage, black and white. The trousers weren't that different, they had many pockets going down the sides of my legs and were closed or rolled up down at the end of the legs. I put 3 of each in the bag and took one grey pullover because I wore another one under my black jeans overall.

While I put underwear for one and a half weeks in my bag, Emma and Isabella realised what I was doing. "Ey mate, what are you doing? Why are you packing?", Emma asked. "Yeah, where are you going?", Isabella followed with the question. "I, I'm just... You know that I never ever have left London and gone to a city which is more than half an hour away. I want to go visit another city, I just want to do that and make a new experience. At school, no one will care and here... you know!", I answered while trying to sound desperate and understandable. "We care! We don't want you to leave, or you take us with you!", Emma said and behind her

Isabella nodded in agreement. But inside my head my brain new that I had to go alone, or I had to explain everything. If I'd explain everything I would sound like a maniac and well, scary. "Guys, it won't be forever. I'm going to come back after a month or so, I don't even know myself. Do you think I could live out there on my own without you? I'll answer: No, I can't! So you just wait here and do what you always wanted to do without me", I proposed but was able to see that they weren't that happy with my idea.

No, Emma didn't seem that happy, but Isabella looked at me and I think she understood that I had to go, so she backed me up and turned around, facing Emma. "She's right! She will have to come back eventually and till then we can listen to rock music as loud as we want, OK?" Emma's expression changed a little, and she eyed me and then Isabella, then sighed. "Fine, but you have to promise to come back as soon as you're done with what ever!" My hand laid on my chest, under which my heart beat strong and full of excitment.

"I promise!"

Chapter 5

I flew over England to north-west, a bird, probably an eagle, was directly next to me. Under us, the earth went from green to grey, from landscape to cities. It was beautiful! I looked over to the eagle again, and it opened its beak. "Help, we need help! Manchester!" I woke up, banged my head on the wooden bar of the bed and fell back into bed. The room was dark, the only source of light came from the window, where the moonlight shone through a slit in the curtain. The light made everything look cold and spooky and the air held a heavy feeling. I took a deep breath and heaved my legs out of my warm and cosy bedsheets.

A breeze let my hair on the neck stand up and touched my arms with its lightness. The floor felt hard and uncomfortable under my skin while I walked over to the window to open it. A wind drove through the room and filled it with fresh, new autumn air. I closed my eyes a second time this night and relaxed my entire body, but just before I dozed of again, my brain said in a small voice in the back. "No, you have to go!" And I knew it was right. I changed into real, warm cloths, took my sport bag and jacket, laid down a letter for Emma and Isabella, then opened the door to a lightly lit hallway, which would lead me to the entrance and from there, finally outside. Still sleep drunk, I followed the hall, to the entry door and stepped into a cold autumn night filled with the smell of rain and thunder. My eyes took a few minutes to adjust to the dark, but after that I was able to see the trees with their little amount of leaves, the buildings of families, the street with its stop signs. My feet carried me down a path and over a crosswalk and ten minutes later another source of light emerged in form of a neon sign of the Londoner underground. My hands were freezing because of the biting cold, so I pulled them a bit further into my selves and continued walking to the station, where the escalator wouldn't start, so that I took the stone steps. The subway station had lights shining and as soon as I sat in one of the waggons, I pulled out my phone on which were the information written: Platform 7; waggon 8A; seat 37; arrival 01:45 o'clock. The subway arrived at 02:15 o'clock, so I had enough time to get myself something to eat and read a chapter of "Because the world doesn't care". The train station of London, wasn't different from many others, it had a huge glass ceiling, shops to buy food, make up and a Harry Potter fan article store. In each platform was a sign or blackboard with information about ones train, for example if it had been delayed. But everything was completely fine. The train to Manchester arrived at exactly 02:45 o'clock, and I was able to find my window seat, where I made myself comfortable. "Three hours and I will find out about the... voices!", I whispered to myself then the engine started, and my view went outside. The streets, cars, buildings, fields and mountains flew by in a blurry rush like in my dream but this time it was real and just beautiful.

The night sky, filled with stars, on the way to Manchester.

Chapter 6

My head banged against the wet glass window, so that I woke up from a dreamless sleep. The speakers in the waggon cracked, and a feminine voice filled the silence: "Dear passengers, we have arrived at our destination. Please leave the waggons and don't forget your luggage. Cari passeggeri..." The woman started talking in Italian and I stood up from my seat, took my bag, howled it onto my back and got outside to the empty platform of the Manchester Piccadilly railway station. It looked smaller than the Londoner station and I just started walking into a direction a sign pointed. The clock showed that it was six o'clock and the first shops had opened, but I decided not to stop but continue walking into the directions of the exit. The ceiling was just like the one in London, made out of glass, so that one could see the sky, but because it was really early and autumn, the sky had still a dark blue as colour. Outside, I followed Fairfield Street towards west, and after 300 metres I turned left.

In front of me, there was the round corner of a

brick building. I was standing infront of a dark oak door with a golden bell glued next to it. I had arrived in my new home, the youth hostel picaddella. There were three floors with 5 windows on each side of the wall. cars of early workers drove by on the Main street, while I waited for someone to open the door I was standing infront and welcome me in. After a minute or so, I heard footsteps approach and a young lady with blond hair opened. "Hello, come in. My name is Clara and I am from germany. Would you like a room to stay?", she asked without having that much of an accent. I went in behind Clara and nodded in agreement. "Yeah, a room would be great. I am probably going to stay here for some days." I said and tried to hide my face, so that Clara would have problems, guessing my age, but I shouldn't have worried, because she was still a bit lazy and told me a room number just After i had payed for three nights. Room number 118, First floor. Upstairs I sneaked into my room, because I didnt want to wake up my new roomates. They snored, so i put down my bag and out door cloths, hung them up and decided to rest a bit longer. But I couldnt dooze of, so that i floated in between sleeping and being awake. After an hour and half or so, one of my companions woke up and went down for breakfast maybe. When I stood up to follow with that Plan, I paused for a second. My body got stiff and the hair on my neck stood up. "Where are we. Please, we will give you anything!" "Oh, someone is scared. You will just have to wait until your parents paid the price for letting us wait." Door slam! My eyes stared into nothing while concentrating on every word. The eco of the voices sounded a bit like a cave and what they have said made me courious. Sweat ran down my back. For me, this had changed some things, while the world continued without noticing. My hunger had gone away completely.

I needed to find these people.

Chapter 7

"Wow, I need to find these people. That's what I thought the whole fricking time, but how? Where were they?", I thought. "And how can they communicate with me? Wait, wait, wait... they can talk to me. What if, I can say something back? Maybe I can find out where they are and who and...okay!" My brain worked Hard and i started going up and down on the yellowish Grass of the Park in Manchester. I had gone there After the voices had talked again, because I needed to get out, get fresh air in my system, and it helped me think. "Okay, okay, soooo... Hello? No, wait. Dear people? No!", I whispered to myself and closed my eyes. I couldn't think about anything to say. I didn't know how to "activate" the whole talking thing. The sun had been up for almost an hour now, but somehow it still felt like night. The trees in the Park had turned themselves from a beautiful green part of the nature into a bald but colourful part of autumn. The leaves had changed their colour into Red and Gold. The sky wasn't blue but White greyish and full of clouds. "I think I got it.

Guys, please here me! My name is Lara and I can somehow hear you. Please try to give me signs and your location, so that I can help you!", I said quietly. Nothing happened, and I gave up all hope of talking to the voices, when I heard a sob. I looked around but no one Was close to me. Some people were walking by in ten metres distance but not a child. "Hello!", the voice said, and I felt relieved. My legs shivered, not because of the cold but because of what i heard next.

"Hey, who are you talking to? Shut up!" The Man who had said that, slapped the child who answered me. It whimpered in pain.

My legs couldn't hold my weight any more and I broke down. The Grass Floor caught my fall. Then i heard the child continue talking, although it got punished before. "Hello, whoever you are. My name is Sam and with me are Val and Eleonore. We are in Manchester in some sort of castle or cave" "or a bunker!", Another child said. "Yeah, maybe a bunker. How, why can you talk to us? Why can you hear us?", they asked me, but I had no answers. I bit my fingernail while thinking about what to say next. A small raindrop fell on me, but I didn't notice. Then i decided, that if someone saw me, talking to myself, they would think I am delusional, so I took out my phone and held it against my cold cheek. "I don't know why I can hear you. I followed your voice to Manchester. I want to help you. Please try to find out where you are and I will come to your help immediately. But one question! How did get caught? Who did it?", I asked and frowned. These were important questions, that needed answers because they could change everything. So I listened and then heard a crack and no one answered me. The connection broke up. Hopefully not forever!

Chapter 8

My mind wasn't ready to go back to the youth hostel or inside at all. It has been 10 minutes since the connection broke down, and I hadn't got a New Signal. The Wind had got stronger and was whistling in my ear. I walked around the City and felt raindrops on my Bair skin, but I didn't care. The children were quiet and didn't talk to me any more, although I tried to contact them again. "A castle or bunker in Manchester", I remembered ad took out my Phone, opened google and looked up: castle Manchester. The First castle that showed itself was called Manchester castle, and you could rent it as a home. But when I wrote Manchester bunker into the Google search System, I got another Name for a place where the children might be kept.

It was called: Worsley New Hall Bunker

When I tried to scroll down and read more about that bunker, I couldn't because of the water that had gathered on the surface of the

Display. So I decided to go get something to eat and then go back to the youth hostel and find out more about the bunker.

I made my way through the streets to a supermarket. My stomach rumbled because I didn't eat all day. Tourist were sightseeing and listened to an elder man, the guide. A family talked with each other in French: "Ce guide sais pas de chose de la ville!"

I had only had taken french for a year, so that I understood some words. I made my way through the crowd and found a bakery where I bought a Sandwich with salad, tomatoes and mozzarella. One if the walls of the bakery was made out of glass, so that I was able to look outside and see the dark and cloudy sky. The raindrops had changed to a waterfall and I could hear thunder in the distance. I sat down on a small wooden table. A homely orange light shone and made the whole room look friendly and warm. The smell of baked goods filled my nostrils and for the first time since I had heard the voices, I was able to relax my body and mind. 14 years old, almost 15 and alone in Manchester, trying to find three children, who had been captured and help them. I took a bite out of my Sandwich and a delicious taste made my hungry stomach go quiet. I closed my eyes and felt the warmth on my arms and I could hear the rain falling on to the (Asphalt), like a rhythm in a song. Then I heard a small crack and felt a wave of... something. The connection was restored, and I was able to hear two words: "Enemy's territory"

Chapter 9

Even though these words weren't answers to my questions, even though they were a bit unsettling, I felt relieved, because the connection still worked and wasn't broken. But I told myself, that I wouldn't talk to Val, Eleonore and Sam right away, so that they wouldn't get into trouble for talking to themselves/me. The rain had got weaker and less, so I said bye to the nice baker's lady who had made my sandwich and went down the Old Mill Street and just followed it for almost a kilometre, then took a small left turn, took a shortcut down a short way through the middle of two buildings, down the A6 and last but not least, a right down the Fairfield Street till I saw the Hostel.

A small part of the sun peeked out from behind the clouds, but that didn't stop the rain, or the wind, but it created a beautiful little rainbow over the city lights and heads of citizens and tourists. The facade of the hostel had changed the colour, from bright red almost pink, to a darker red, like wine. The door wasn't locked while daytime, so I pulled it open on the golden door handle, then cleaned my shoes on the doormat with the silly picture of a cat printed on. My eyes scanned the room for Clara, but I didn't find her but another Person who wore the same Uniform of the youth hostel. From the name tag which was pinned to his chest, was the name, Jaidan. "Hello, ähm... Jaidan. I wanted to know if you have a computer where I could look some things up, or WiFi?", I asked when he had reached earshot. "Oh, sure. There is a community computer right over there. Just don't go on any suspicious Websites or you know", he answered helpfully and winked at me, then turned away and walked to an elder man with backpack and grandchildren. I smiled and sat down on the chair in front of the computer. The password was written on a sticky note which hanged at the black display. My fingers flew over the keyboard and seconds later I was reading about the Worsley New Hall Bunker and its history. While reading, I focused only on the words and excluded the rest o the World. But then a loud group of wet and cold students who went backpacking entered and filled the whole entry with noise. I was annoyed and tried to cut out everything again, so that I were able to proceed with research. Till then, I had found out, that the bunker had been build by the war department, for employees. It was abandoned and now out of use for most of the time. "So a perfect place to hide three kid- napped children!"

The sky had darkened again, lightning struck, thunder only seconds after. They had to be there. They had to be there!

Chapter 10

I sat in front of the computer for another hour and looked up different information about the bunker's history, the underground stations close to it, and sometimes I picked up my phone and pretended to talk to a family member, but actually was trying to reach out to Sam. It was exhausting!

The next day I woke up after a good night of sleep. The bags under my eyes had gone back, and I felt like something important would happen that morning.

I stood up, brushed my teeth, put cloths on and ate a Croissant for breakfast. After that I took a smaller bag and filled it with important stuff I might need for exploring and/or finding and rescuing the three children. So I took a rope, a torch, a knife I had stolen from Emma who got it from her girlfriend, but didn't know what to do with it. Also, I put in a bottle of water, a map, money and two apples I had got from the entry table of the hostel.

So when I was all set, I made my way through the entrance room, where new people had arrived, down the main street, to an underground Station. From there I took a subway to the place called "The Coppice", or well, near that place.

The area had changed a lot, but I tried to stay positive. "At least the weather isn't as bad as yesterday!", I told myself while walking to a gate which would lead to the old bunker. My heart rate went up while I went inside the area. It wasn't forbidden to go there but if there were the children, then there probably also were the people who had captured them. But I tried to block out these thoughts and concentrate on the surrounding nature. The trees and bushes were covered in dew and glittered in the weak sunshine. The ground under my feet was light and bouncy, but also full of wet red, orange and yellow leaves. The path was out of gravel and dirt, surrounded by dead bushes and after some metres, it split. I decided to take a right turn and while continuing walking, I was able to see Ruins of the old building which stood here before it was destroyed.

The whole surroundings were a bit spooky and the Ruins looked like a place that Zombies and ghosts would haunt. The weather didn't make it better, and the wind that sounded like a person whispering quietly right into my ear. A chill ran down my spine and goosebumps appeared on both, arms and legs.

I was wandering around the area until, after about an hour or longer, I saw a grey quader mate out of concrete and steel. The bunker. On the walls were colourful paintings sprayed on with gravities, names of the artists, eyes, faces or just symbols in every colour existing.

But after years of being left alone, the stone had been overgrown by the nature. Tendrils and moss grew up the walls and made everything look more wild and own minded. The bunker looked cold, unfriendly and like it shouldn't be entered. I walked around the Quader, looking for a way to get inside. But the nature didn't make it easier, the path that had led me through the forest in the area, had disappeared and had been replaced by 1 to 1.5 metre high bushes and branches. Over me, birds sang a song, which sounded dark and grim. "Wow, even the birds think I am going to die!" I laughed to release the feeling of unease. But somehow, I couldn't shake of the feeling of being followed. Like someone was watching me.

Chapter 11

After climbing over the natures obstacles, I found a "door" to get inside. The first time I saw it, everything was full of stones and I couldn't even go near the entry, but on the exact other side of the quader, there was the entry copied, but without the stones, only the doorway. I climbed over the last thing blocking the way and sneaked up onto the door. I heard a notice from behind me, but wasn't able to see anything or anyone. "Probably an animal or so!", I told myself reassuringly. Then I pulled out my torch from the small bag I had packed earlier that day. It would come in handy now, because first, the sun was on its way down, and second, the bunker didn't have any electricity, so no light and no windows for light to shine in. I take a small peak around the corner of the doorway and saw black. It was pitch-black!

My heart rate increased, and I closed my eyes for two seconds, in which I told myself: "It's fine. We just need to find the children!" So I stepped around the corner and went inside the black hole.

As soon as I stepped inside, I lit my torch and a middle large circle of light glided over the inner walls, which were also full of gravity. My normal breath, sounded louder than usual, my steps sounded louder than usual. The floor was made out of concrete, and every step I took echoed through the place. After a couple of minutes in the bunker, I felt how my eyes adjusted to the small amount of light coming from the blue light of the torch, I held. I took one step after the other and slowly arrived at the other end of the first room. My eyes saw two ways, one that went left, and one that had a right turn. Left and right continued on the same floor. The left turn was more open and didn't have that many bricks and stones in the way. The right way somehow, got even darker than before. After only a couple of metres, it turned left, so that I wasn't able to see, what was behind the dark corner.

Obviously I took the right and scary way. Around the corner, a completely New room opened up, but it had only two ways parting from it. The one I was standing on, and another one at the south West side of the room. I could hear a light beeping Sound in my ear. My tinnitus kicked in hard, but I tried to ignore it and proceed with my plan. My feet carried my body to the south-west wall, where steps led down into the basement. "Shit, well, shit. Ahhh!", I whispered to myself so quietly, that even with the echo, only people with great hearing would hear my sentence. The torch lit down the steps and lit up the ground at the bottom. I walked down the stairs with new-found determination. I followed the corridor till another crosswalk showed up. I decided to do a trick. "Right, then left, ten right, then left!" So I took a left turn. The bunker air was cold, and I felt relieved, that I had taken my warm pullover with me. The air smelt like rain, wet stones, and mud. I proceeded walking down the muddy corridor, witch the torch dancing over the walls, and had sunken into my thoughts of being in every other possible place, than this one. Then I heard a noise.

Chapter 12

The Echo carried the noise, so that it sounded like it was right next to me. My breathing got harder and faster. "OK, OK, it's fine. The noise, it must be the rain or a racoon. It is fine!" But I didn't believe myself. I pressed my back against the wall of the hallway, which was a tactical smart thing to do, because no one was able to attack me from behind. The wall was, like ever other part of the bunker, made out of concrete, riddled with steel. The texture was rough and felt like a Peeling. Sweat ran down my neck and into my pullover. Before, I was happy to have a pullover, because of the cold air and breeze, but now my body sent heat away from me, and it gathered in my pullover. Before continuing walking, I looked left and right and let the torch glide over the walls, floor and ceiling.

When I was sure, that no one was following me, I made myself do another step and then another one. I walked and took alternately a left turn and a right turn.

Arrived in a new part, the smell had changed. The air was stuffy and smelt like vomit. I tried to breathe as much through my mouth as I could, and pulled a piece of clothing in front of my nose. This time, the room had four different directions, each with a new corridor parting off. I went over to the first and shined inside. A long hallway just going in one direction. The second resembled the first, but after circa 20 metres, it took a left turn and a right.

Then I walked to the third doorway and didn't see anything. There was another corridor with a staircase at the end of it. It went even further down, but I was able to see, that the passage was blocked with stone quaders.

The last doorway also had a staircase. It went up, but not to the same level, as in the beginning, but to a new level, which was in the middle of the first floor and the basement. I would have taken the first way, but as soon as I turned away from the fourth, I saw something, that changed my mind. A light. Not the one from my weak torch. No, a light that came from the middle level. Then I heard Sam's voice in my head. "Hello, where are you?", he asked, but

I realised something different again. The voice was in my head but a second after, an Echo whispered in my ear: Hello, where are you? It was the same question and the same voice that was in my head. But this time, it came from the level above me.

I had found them!

Chapter 13

The weak orange light shone from above me, so I followed it up the stairs and peaked around the wall on the right side. The view that opened up to me was breathtaking in a bad way. I had never seen Val, Eleonore and Sam, but I knew that the children, who were captured and sitting in front of me, that they were them. Sam's question was still in my head, but I didn't dare answering, because the people who had captured them, might have been able to hear me.

The three children were full of mud and one girl had wound, where the blood had built a crust. Val and Eleonore where two girls, one had brown curly hair, the other blonde straight hair. Both must have been around twelve years old, and Sam didn't look that much older. He had middle long brown, black hair and looked like thirteen or fourteen years old.

The three looked thin, tired, and like they hadn't seen the sunlight in days, and they didn't think they ever would. So that they couldn't run away, they were tied up with chains and a rope. Then I looked around in the big room, to see if the kidnappers were guarding them. The room must have filled up most of the middle floor, because it was huge. Not in height, but in length. There was a camping table placed in the middle, with camping chairs around it. The light I saw, emerged from a lightbulb on the ceiling and another source was a torch, that lay on the table in the middle.

Two people, a man, maybe 40 years old, and a woman, about 35 years old, were wandering around the room. The man kept an eye on the children, so that they could not even talk to each other. The woman read newspapers. "Ey, Mathew! They search for the children in an area close to us. Should we worry?", she said with concern in her voice, while she walked over to the man, so-called Mathew. He looked at the papers and answered: "Nee, that's fine. We will call the parents and threaten them again. Maybe send a bloody cloth or something, so that they finally understand, that we are dead serious!" The woman nodded with excitement, looked down at the children and laughed a villain laugh. They continued walking around and sometimes talking to each other, while I knelled in the shadows of the corner, trying to figure out a plan for me to rescue the three, without getting noticed, or if noticed, that we have a fast way out.

"Please, Lara! They want to hurt us. Bunker, Manchester!"I couldn't figure out if he had talked in my head, or if I heard the sentence from 10 metres before me. They sounded desperate, and scared. How Sam had managed to talk to me without the kidnappers to hear him, I didn't know, but I wanted to tell them that I was there. "If I tell them, they might look at me and the bad guys will see me, but they need to know, that I am here, and that I want to help them escape!", I thought, but didn't need to decide for myself, because right when I compared my options, a strong hand grabbed me with an iron grip.

Chapter 14

Panic! I quickly turned my head around to see the person who caught me. It was a man, with short, black hair that stood up from his head, a scar under his chin and yellow eyes, which smiled with proud of catching me. "Hey, Mathew, Jolin! I found someone!" The man behind me pushed me in the dim lit room, where his two comrades stood, waiting for us.

I looked to the Val and the others who had confusion in their eyes. I saw Sam's lips move and heard his voice in my head. "Are you with us right now?" I gave a slight nod, which no one except the children saw. "What are you doing here? Are you spying on us? Is there anyone else here? Who did you tell?", Jolin, the woman, screamed at me, while I looked up at him with a completely straight face. "Why do you have three small children captured and chained up?", I asked them strongly and without fear. "Hey, you don't ask the questions!", Mathew said with raised voice and hit me with his hand across my face. I felt my cheek sizzle and it hurt bad.

The man who had found me, didn't loosen his grip around my shoulder and noodled two the woman. She said: "Mat, take the girl for a second!" He followed the order and the black haired man and middle-aged woman walked a bit away from us to talk, which didn't really help. I still understood every word that was said. "What should we do? What if the girl had someone with her?" "We will tie her up, throw her to the other stupid kids. But before we must find out if someone was with her, you are right!" The woman walked back over to us, while the man took a rope from the table in the middle. While he was on his way to us, the woman started talking to me. "Is there someone with you?" I didn't answer, because I would have more time to figure out an escape plan, while questioning. Jolin took her hand, flung it and slapped me on the not already slapped cheek. I closed my eyes, because of the pain, but tried to look neutral on the outside. "How did you find us?", she asked. I didn't answer and this time the man hit me, because he had given Mathew the rope, to tie me up. They continued asking the same questions over and over again, while Mathew tried to get my hands into slings.

Then I saw something absurd. That's when I thought I started hallucinating. There were three girls, one with brown hair, one with brown-black hair and one with really blonde hair. Not Val and Eleonore, but Isabella and Emma and I think Emma's girlfriend! I looked away, so that if they were real, I wouldn't lead the kidnappers to them, but from the corner my eyes, I saw that they were untying them and Emma's girlfriend, Alex, had pulled out a lock pick from her pocket. Emma, Isabella and Alex freed Sam and Val quietly, then turned to help to Eleonore out of her chains. The two children who were freed, sat still, and didn't make a move, so that no one would see them, while my three friends from London sneaked to Eleonore. But when Isabella took a chain, it jingled and the echo of the huge room carried the small noise to the three people surrounding me. All of them turned around quickly and saw... six teenagers, ready to fight for each other.

Chapter 15

Even though I was in a bad position, I felt proud and full of new hope. "Maybe, we will be able to go out as winners today! Maybe", I thought and couldn't keep it in me any more. I laughed, I felt relieved, we were saved, not by anyone random, no, by my dearest friends. Our enemies didn't think that was funny.

The man, who I found out seconds later, was called Livon. "Livon, grab them!", Jolin screamed with rage. He obeyed and ran to my friends. They screamed at each other and everyone ran into a different direction, which led o complete chaos. I jumped up, with my hands tied to my back and tried to run to Emma, but Mathew blocked my way. He was bigger than I thought and also more muscular, but I kicked him first to his leg, then in his middle area. He crouched in pain. "One down!", I thought proudly and ran to Emma, who punched me to the shoulder. "You will need to explain all of this!", she threatened, and I nodded but replied: "Same for you!"

But in the middle of our little conversation we were interrupted by a gun shot. Jolin, the woman in her mid-thirties, held up a black hand pistol, which every bad guy in a fim uses. She had fired a warning shot at the ceiling, were a bullet hole appeared. "So, everyone. You stupid children will put away your weapons, come to us and do not think about doing something against us! Or I will use this pistol, I promise, i won't hesitate for a second!" And I knew that she said the truth.

In seconds, everything had turned to something good for us, and seconds after, we were facing our defeat again. Like a roller-coaster. A roller-coaster that was playing with lives.

My hands were still behind my back, bonded with thick ropes, so that I wasn't able to hold up my hands in defeat. So I got on my knees as a sign for cooperation. Sam and his friends held up their hands too, but not the Londoners. They stood there like strong trees without flinching, and just full of strength. "Ohh, if I were you, I would put down the gun, go on the knees next to your companions", Alex pushed Livon to her, and he fell on his knees. His face was red like a tomato, because he had realiced, that he was beaten up by a couple of children. "Before we entered, we called the police! They are going to arrive here in about a minute. If you give us the weapon, and we tie you up, we will say, that you cooperated."

Jolin's face changed from hard and angry to scared, measuring and a little bit disgusted. It was, as if you could see her thoughts, her brain trying to figure out, if Emma, Alex and Isabella were lying or telling the truth, which would mean, that, if they were telling the truth, she had to find a fast way out. "I am not lying! Give us your weapon, and you might end up with one or two years less in jail" And as if everything was planned, two men in police uniform, and with guns in their hands, sprinted in the room.
"Hands up, you are arrested! Everything you say, can and will be used against you!"

Chapter 16

"Laraaaa!" I heard my name being screamed. I turned around and was blended by the sun, and run over by my old roommates. "How dare you run away and not tell us, that you wanted to have an adventure!", Emma said with happiness glowing from her whole body.

"How did you know about the three children who where captured?", Isabella asked, and at this question Emma went quiet.

I shook my head and pointed to a side next to the bunker, where fewer people were running around, and we could talk in private. They followed me there, and we sat down in a circle on the forest ground. "So, I guess you have many questions and I decently have some too. I will start, cause as soon as Emma starts talking, she can't stop!" We all laughed, and before we started discussing the serious stuff, I just let myself feel relieved and happy to be around my friends.

"So, everything started the day I ran away" And I told them everything. Every little detail, about the voices, where I stayed, till the moment they showed up. And they believed me! They asked some questions like, which voice did you hear, or was it creepy! I answered and they seemed happy with my answers. "But now, my question! How did you find me?"

"Woah, OK! Well, we saw you packing your stuff that day and thought: Hey what's up with her? Does she want to run away? So we decided to pack as well, so that when you ran away in the middle of the night, we could follow you. And we did! We took the same train you took, just sat in another compartment, we slept in the same house you did, without you noticing. We followed you everywhere you went, but didn't want to tell you, because you looked worried and up to something. And we thought you found out about us, when you were about there...", Emma pointed at the bush, where I went inside the bunker, then took a deep breath and continued, "But you didn't, and when you were captured by this dude", she pointed at Livon, "We had to do something! Ahh, and we told Alex about everything, because she is strong and well, good, soooo, yeah!"
Isabella just nodded and I laughed. "Thank god for you being so creepy!" We all started giggeling, but then a police officer came over to

us and stopped our chitchat by saying: "Sam, Valerie and Eleonore would like to talk to you, Lara!"

Sam and the others sat on the edge of the hospital car. They looked up and Sam said without hesitation: "I don't know you, but you and your friends saved our lives and I will always, forever be grateful! But I have a question, which is bothering me. Why can I talk to you in my head?" That was a question that had been bothering me too, and it wasn't easier for me, because I didn't have an answer. "I don't know?", I said and Sam looked down at his feet, slightly disappointed, but understanding. "How is your face?", Valerie, or short Val, asked me with a smile. "It's good, thank you!", I answered and smiled back at her. "Sam", I turned to look at him again," I don't know why we can talk to each other, but I want to find out, so this is my telephone number, and please call me, or well, talk to me, soon, okay?" He nodded and we looked at each other.

We both had a connection, and didn't understand why. Then I said my goodbyes, and a police officer drove my friends and me back to London. When I entered the car, I felt something rip inside me!

Thank you

I want to thank my amazing friend and editor, Corinne Alyssa Klarmann, for helping me, edit my book, and for helping me, when I was out of words, out of ways to make my story appear real.

I also want to thank my siblings and my parents, who helped me on the way, by encouraging me.

Without my friends, I couldn't have written this book either. They didn't only help me to bring the characters to life, by giving them their names, but also their appereance.

The last people I want to thank, are you, for reading this. For making this happen, and making me happy, by just reading these lines and all the lines before.

Thank you, and everyone in the process!

AVA SCHREIBER

Ava Schreiber was born in 2010 in Munich.
She grew up in germany and attends a grammar school
there too.
Shehad started writing stories and poems at the age of 11
and competed in writing competitions in her school.

Loved this book?
Why not write your own at story.one?

Let's go!